DEEP OVERSTOCK

#22: Knots
October 2023

NAUT - KNOTS

EDITORIAL

EDITORS-IN-CHIEF: Mickey Collins & Robert Eversmann

MANAGING EDITOR: Z.B. Wagman

POETRY: Timothy Arliss OBrien, Jihye Shin & Nicholas Yandell

PROSE: Z.B. Wagman

COVER: "Rope" ca. 1550–1295 B.C., on display at The Met

CONTACT: editors@deepoverstock.com
deepoverstock.com

Letter from the Editors

Dearest Readers,

You've been knotty, haven't you? Just a little? That's ok. We've tied all of that up into a neat little journal here.

Don't worry, we won't string you along. Please enjoy the knot pieces within *Deep Overstock 22*. We have poems (and a couple prose pieces) all about how knots, and ropes, and strings, and twine bring us together, or keep us apart.

But we're hoping that knot even death will keep you from submitting to our next issue: *Ghosts*. We want ghosts of Christmas future (it's just around the corner), ghosts that moan and howl, ghosts of past lovers, or forgotten lunches. Give us your scary ghosts or your friendly ghosts. Whatever haunts your halls, send them our way. We'll bust 'em. Submit your ghoulish work by November 30th.

You can't tie us down,

Deep Overstock Editors

In the Beginning
by Lynette Esposito

The heavy night
opened her womb
and the earth was born--
a beautiful baby blue and green
held together with
delicate knots woofed
on an invisible loom--
swaddling a new star in the universe.

knot tying
by Mark DeCarteret

not that one takes a bow
after every two lines

this body mostly water
now spoke of in halves

or raise one finger after four
give ourselves an extra hand after six

but one might celebrate quietly after eight
this body mostly air now imperfectly squared

Bowline
by Rin Stone

I would sit in the blazing Alabama heat with my cousins.

Picking nectarines from my great aunt's tree.

I must have swallowed a pit,
Since I've had a knot in my stomach since I was 10.

Or maybe the pit wasn't the first knot.

Maybe the fermented juice running down my chin wouldn't be
the only pleasure that would also cause me pain.

It could have been on my 8th birthday when we were on our
way to my favorite restaurant,
When the crunched remains of our car crushed me so small
that my intestines tied themselves together.

Or maybe it was when my teacher found out I couldn't tie my
shoes.

I could read at a high school level but couldn't tie my laces
because my head was too busy reciting the varieties of knots it
had tied my stomach in.

Every time she told me to look her in the eye, it learned a new
one.

Or perhaps it was when my first girlfriend showed me how to
tie a cherry stem with my tongue before I stammered out "I love
you"

Before she reached far enough to tug on the nectarine pit.

Careful to tangle herself into every knot on the way.

I still have a hard time telling pleasure from pain.

The Secret Guest

by Nicholas Yandell

(with a nod to Rumi)

The you I once knew is tied up in a basement. It's dark and cold and isolated from view. When I illuminate your body, with a candle's flicker, and the knots that bind you to that sturdy wooden chair, I can't let myself stay too long.

This extended liminal space was never meant to be your resting place, but I knew no other options. I bound up your memory, with strands of restraint, for my safety... as my vice. And though it's been so long since we last touched, I still feel your movements resisting the ropes. They're rubbing against your skin, with a slow burn of friction, across the span of time.

I too am bound, with long cords, around my wrists, on my ankles, in my stomach, and my throat. They keep me dangled over the precipice, of never knowing where I'll be, without your shell to cling. For you may have the same body, and the same soul, but nothing else has stayed so firmly consistent. Left imprisoned and deprived of light, just so I can revisit your past existence.

But no longer will I have you, as a prisoner in my depths. This is the last time I'll come to that lonely room. As a pilgrimage of release, I'll sever your bindings and set you free. And long after the cords have fallen away, you'll still occasionally drift through me, but with rays of elucidation, revealing what you'll always be: A memory of happenings that altered me chemically... far beyond ephemeral reality.

When you return though, at future hours, I'll set a room to welcome you, as my honored guest for a moment or two. However long you stay, there will be comfortable chairs, with no constraint, where we can commune in harmony. And when you're finished and ready to leave, I'll simply smile and say goodbye, releasing you into the night, as a memento from another time.

With passing years and changing needs, in a flow of dwindling frequency, I'll still be grateful for your presence. As a guide in the winding journey, to know my secret guests and the part they play in me. Through an act of liberation, a gift of illumination, and the possibilities each open door can bring.

Initial Contact
by Yuan Changming

The only reason Ming had traveled across the whole Pacific Ocean from Vancouver to Lotus Village was, hopefully, to see Chiung for the first and last time after he left his native place more than half a century ago.

However, upon arrival, he found himself a total stranger. While no villager could recognize him or tell him anything about those he'd used to hang around with after school, the familiar river marking the village boundary had dried up completely. From a distant relative, he learned that Chiung had married someone from a neighboring town and brought up a couple of children before she died of some disease in her forties. Other than these few vague facts, nobody could really remember who she was or what she had done, but Ming believed that there must have been many heart-wrenching cries over her loss, though none of them had anything to do with him. Definitely not. For he had already died even before her, on a sleepless autumn night, when he quietly buried his young heart under the village's tallest banyan tree before his relocation. Now the whole village has taken on a new look, the tree had long gone with the wind, their muted laughs traceable only between the rings of the stump, which was still visible like an old scar on a newly lifted face.

Strictly speaking, Chiung was not his first love, nor could he recall exactly how it all began and ended, but she was the first girl who had come into physical contact with him in his lifetime.

It was probably in the early summer of 1971. Just a couple of months earlier, he'd had his initial experience of spermatorrhea. Thinking that he'd unknowingly wetted his bed like a toddler, he became so deeply ashamed of himself that he decided to keep this incident as his darkest secret. Since no one had taught him anything about puberty, his sexual ignorance was certainly forgivable, though he did begin to enjoy looking at pretty girls like Chiung, a classmate whose family lived in the same part of the village. Slim, fair-skinned, with a conspicuous tear birthmark on her left cheek, about two years older and half a head taller than himself, she was the best-looking girl in his school.

Despite their close contact, he never asked her why she liked him. Probably because living with his relatives as a foster child, he was different from all other normal village boys. More probably because he was silly in a good-natured way; for instance, when their Chinese teacher ridiculed him for being the lousiest composition writer in the class, he laughed together with all others as if the teacher had been talking about someone else. Most probably because he had somehow received more attention from teachers than he should otherwise have deserved: for instance, within a month after they began to attend junior high school, he was hand-picked by the music teacher to play an important role in the school theatre. On several occasions, he did want to ask her how they two had "come together," but to honor her quiet character, he refrained from raising this question.

No matter the reason, each time he felt like meeting her in person, he would loudly sing a particular line from the drama in the classroom to signal his request, "Be there or be square." As previously agreed, she would go and wait on the river bank until he joined her for the twilight tryst. Then he would snuggle in her arms like a small puppy for as long as they both wanted. In the meantime, they would say nothing, let alone do anything more than hold each other tightly. The most unforgettable act they performed together was to watch stars appearing in the sky as it was getting darker minute by minute. When there were thick clouds hanging above their heads, they would just listen to the reeds swinging against the wind as if to keep any trespasser far away from them. Chiung might well have had some sexual whims, but she never yielded to them, if any at all, while it never crossed his mind to touch her face or any other part of her body with his hands. He could have done whatever he was up to, including kissing her on the lips or even fucking her in wildness, but just as his young body was not ready for sex yet, his heart still remained as un-polluted as the water in the Lotus River. What he yearned for most back then was some tangible tenderness from a female he really liked, something which he found not only physically attractive but spiritually soothing.

On a late mid-summer evening, he and Chiung spent more time than usual sitting on a sandy ridge in front of a long stretch of flowering reeds. For the first twenty minutes or so, they just kept listening to the songs of frogs and cicadas. With her long arms embracing him tightly from behind, he could smell her unique girlishness as he imagined himself taking a bath in her water-like femininity. For a moment, he heard her breathing heavily and even felt her heart beating against his naked back, which made him wonder if she was going to swoop on him like a big estrous female cat.

This situation reminded him how, when he visited one of his aunts in the previous summer, her female cat clutched at his left thigh and would tighten its claw whenever he attempted the slightest movement. To prevent it from hurting him more, he had to play dead for the whole night until it loosened its grasp at daybreak.

A few days later, Ming had to leave the village to join his parents in New Rivermouth, the biggest town in the county. Since that sudden move, he's never seen Chiung again, but always remembers her, even long after the entire world has long forgotten her.

NE Knott 2700 St

DNA AND
by Aletha Irby

Eugene & Eugenia
On their honeymoon
Finally entwined
In the ampersand
Which separated
The italic lettering
Of their names
On wedding invitations
Supersede
The eugenics initiatives
Of sansevieria-tongued mothers-in-law
Eugenia's ovum
A planet-sized Gordian Knot
Which Eugene's spermatozoon
Pierces like Alexander's sword
To procreate the jejune Euphrosyne
Who nonetheless will evolve rapidly
To befriend textile and tektite
Both terrestrial
And extraterrestrial texts
Who eschewing Iphigenian virtues
An Aegean Agamemnon's
Drunken narcissistic blues
Will subject herself
To the syncopated clairaudience
Of her only unbidden muse

Medusa's Love Story

by Lynette Esposito

She stared at me with her marble eyes
and knotted my heart so tight
it turned to splintered stone—
pieces pierced my soul
and turned it as well.
Then—now, I am alone--
unmarked granite
above a grave not yet dug.

Boating Knots
by Paul Hostovsky

My stepson only eats hamburgers
and fries. And chicken nuggets.
Nary a vegetable or piece of fruit. And why
doesn't he get scurvy and die?

He never goes outside. Zero
exposure to the sun. Just stays in his room
playing video games all day. And why
doesn't he get rickets and die?

Just look at his room–he hasn't
cleaned it in over a year. His socks
are so defiled you could stand them up
and watch them defile out the door.

The toxic waste under his bed alone
should have killed him years ago.
Don't misunderstand me, I don't
wish him dead. But if he sailed away

on a long sea journey, say,
stuck on board for months on end
with no land in sight and nothing
to do all day but practice

his boating knots, I wouldn't
miss him. I would wish him
bon voyage and give him a lemon
as a parting gift, for the vitamin C,

if only for his mother's sake.

The Sea
by James G. Piatt

The raucous sea, far below
an outgrowth of colorful flowers
wafting fragrances into the air,
its undulant swelling movement
carries the tide surging toward shore,
its waves heaved high into the air,
with splashes of briny teal,
topped with white whiskers,
like an old man with his restlessness.

Icarus's Wings
by Ben Macnair

Icarus had told Eeyore they could never be friends
'Eeyore, I am not like you, not like you at all,
I have no time for self-pity, no time to stop and stare,
I need to build these wings and take to the air.

Eeyore had felt sad.
He knew that Icarus saw the sky as something to conquer,
To master, he wanted to fly, to soar.
Eeyore saw the sky as only grey.
He only really noticed it when it rained,
He only knew a journey began, when he was on the train.

Icarus told his old friend he would never know how it felt to be free.
He had never had the imagination to see past his own nose.
He would only see the naked Emperor, and never his new clothes.
Eeyore only ever saw the consequences.
If he started a conversation with somebody new,
He would remember never to talk to strangers.

Icarus only saw the possibilities.
He saw the sky as something new to conquer.
He never saw the ground as something to fear.
Icarus built his wings, he wanted to touch the Sun,
He wanted to experience the warmth of a solar flare.
He wanted to feel unencumbered by the ground,
By everybody's expectations.
He wanted his name to be remembered in Posterity,
He wanted his name to echo through the whole of eternity.

Eeyore never had the chance to warn his friend.
Eeyore had never known the exhilaration of touching the moon,
But he had known the pain of gravity,
Returning him too fast, and too soon.

speed reading
by Mark DeCarteret

not that I clove to you
like a ghostly sheet, love

rolled my tongue into an O
or another self, taut as a clothesline,

some caricature bent to my likeness
or some trucker's star hitched

half to the wind, half to the little
pill slipped under their tongues

JOSH
Le Bontemps
Café & Catering
Bon Appetit!
NE Knott 2700 St
THIS BLOCK
PUSH BUTTON FOR WALK SIGNAL
WARNING

Knots
by Timothy Arliss OBrien

I am tying myself into knots. I undo them and redo them.

I am myself knots. I undo and redo.

I am knots. I undo them.

I knot myself. Undo and redo.

I am tying knots into myself.

I redo and undo and undo and redo.

I am myself, tying myself into knots.

I am knoting myself, into and undo.

I am knots and I redo myself.

Tying myself into myself: I am knots.

I am tying myself into knots.

Anniversary
by Lynette Esposito

They stood before the priest and knotted
themselves together with a vow
until death do us part.
And yet, what if the knot
stays tight and death is
just an illusion
of escape?

Cat Karma
by Yuan Changming

"Definitely, I must have a mystic connection with cats," Ming concluded. Otherwise, he could never understand why he'd nurtured such a strong ambivalence about the creature. On the one hand, he liked a cat's handsome face, its quiet character, its soft and light movements as well as its grooming habit, but on the other hand, he seemed to have an innate fear of cats, though he was not born in the year, or with the psychology, of the rat, which dare not play unless the cat's away.

It was during the summer holidays of 1969 when he'd just finished elementary school. He was visiting his step-aunt living in a faraway village. For a whole week, the weather was sizzling hot, even in the evening. To get some sleep, he lied down on a door board laid flat in the front yard of her house, almost totally naked, hoping to get a bit of coolness of the night. He was dreaming about playing in the bamboo grove when he felt a sudden sharp. Between wake and sleep, he perceived a cat clutching at his left thigh. He tried to get rid of it, but each time he attempted the slightest movement, he felt the cat tightening its grasp. After many trials and failures, he decided to give up, waiting passively for the cat to loosen its grip of its own accord. During this endless process, he was nervous and stressed, over-whelmed with a sense of agony, but he had to endure the torture inflicted on him by the cat. He didn't know why the creature had picked him and what it wanted from him, nor could he tell later for sure if this incident was just a nightmare or a true experience, but that was the time when he began to avoid the creature like an evil spirit.

Later on, he heard people say that one of the most expensive dishes in traditional Cantonese cuisine was called 'Dragon and Tiger Fight," a course prepared with the meat of a cat and that of a snake as the two major ingredients. In folk culture, the cat represented the tiger, while the snake stood for the dragon. "So, a cat can be cooked as a meat dish," he felt amazed at the idea.

As if karma would have it, he had another close contact with the creature when he started to attend senior high school. It was during a field trip to a hilly village where Ming and his classmates were dispatched to "learn farming" according to Chairman Mao's teachings. On a dark evening, his teacher caught a wild cat somewhere and challenged all the boys to act like Wu Song, the nationally popular hero portrayed in the famous classic novel Outlaws of the Marsh, who killed a tiger with his bare hands. Partly to strengthen his guts and partly to seek revenge for the hurt he got, Ming offered to do the bloody job. With a big knife in his hand, his eyes tightly closed, he held his breath and chopped the cat's head off. After giving him a whole pile of compliments, the teacher taught him to skin it and then cooked its meat with a lot of turnip slices. "This way, the soup and meat wouldn't taste sour," he told the boys. "But don't eat the turnips, for they would have an awful taste after absorbing all the bad flavor."

However, Ming did not like the dish at all. The meat was very special, as it contained no fat but countless thin layers of muscle tissues. Imagining how the headless cat might have looked, he couldn't help feeling like throwing out. Worse still, he just couldn't erase the memory of this experience though he longed to, especially after he learned that it's bad luck to kill such "spirited" creatures as cats, snakes and turtles.

As he grew older, he learned to do good deeds like Liao-fan, one of his most famous ancient ancestors who kept improving his fortune by performing a kind act on a daily basis. In following his example, Ming hoped he could also attain an equilibrium between yin and yang or maintain a balance within his life. He knew that he must do something about his murder of an innocent creature, or else he was fated to be punished in one way or another, sooner or later.

However, he was never sure if he could do enough to atone for his evilness, but as he realized now, the three women he had loved with his heart and soul in his life, namely, Hua, his first crush and lifelong soulmate, Yiming, his first date who caused him almost to commit suicide, and Helen, his beloved wife, each looked like a cat in a different way.

String

by Emily J. Schnipper

(after Henry Darger's collection, as told by Olivia Laing)

amazing how
bits of string
connect the days
darn up the weak spots
entertain the eye
flower in a dark room
gutter rescued
handled carefully
imagine being threaded through a city
just as you were falling apart
knots to puzzle over at night
lines crossing lines, patterning
myriad layers appearing as
nesting material for dreams
obsessive collecting
pacifies the danger
quiets the bad thoughts
reliable old twine
sewing songs of delight
tools of repair in hand
until you've really loved an object
vowed to protect it
whole worlds remain unseen
xenial, precious string
yoked to a kind of survival
zippering the broken heart

Wake
by Kai Broach

A scar, a score
it spews, egg-white from satin blue
infinitude,   idly sliced through
by some passenger,   determined voyager.

So quickly,   it fades
rippling, the thread
reknits, repaired.
The dream is whole again.
And of the voyager nothing remains
but a gentle crease along the waves.

emotional whispers

by James G. Piatt

i found a discarded memory

in the blueness

of my mind

it was covered with

an outgrowth of a

child that lived

in a treehouse

covered with a protrusion of green

it was in the wee hours

of that foggy morning

when small birds

created new songs

from old images

sketched from the projection

of knotted twine from their nest

painted with

emotional whispers

that was an outgrowth of

of their love

NE Knott 2700 St
STOP

Forced

by Angela Townsend

Do I force it?

Do I yank the words to their feet when they are tired and hungry?

Do I prime the pump with docile paragraphs, cat stories for work and case studies in my neuroses?

Do I trust that the main thing is the meeting itself, woman and words, moon and sea, hour and honesty?

Do I press my face to the glass, hold my heart in a teacup, risk rejection by language itself?

The time will pass anyway. I take note of the brain fog advisory. I can see as far as my next comma.

The Divine Mercy figurine grips His heart on my desk. He can hear my prayers. He can share them with my father and grandfather, who I invoke for help with writing and living.

I make pilgrimage to their photograph. I feel certain that they are invested in this, smiling from 1986 in their DADDY and GRANDADDY T-shirts.

But my brain is bankrupt today, and dare I keep harassing the keys? How do I tell the ancient story, that riot of reassurance and reckless love, when I can't even tell what I'm doing here?

Where does the light go when my stories go nowhere? Is there value in the vapid, some brothy nourishment when the words roll away like Spaghetti-O's?

I write a paragraph and erase it. I hook all my highlighters together like grappling hooks.

I read the bottle of glucose tablets on my desk. The glucose copywriter is gifted beyond me. The tablets tell a story far clearer than my pudding. NATURAL GRAPE FLAVOR. CHEW COMPLETELY. CONSULT WITH HEALTHCARE PROFESSIONAL TO DETERMINE BEST SERVING SIZE.

But my eyes are bigger than my stomach, and I consult no one. I stamp my feet and dance the tarantella. I can't see over the top of the winepress. I can't see where this is leading. Grapes bounce off in all directions. I envy everyone who has ever been able to write in any clear direction.

I only know that I need to keep this appointment, this hairy hour of obligation. The dry creekbed reminds me that flow is gift. The burning breaking my heart reminds me that there is still fire.

The fact that I need this when it hates me tells me that love is stronger than ego.

My father wrote a secret novel, yellow legal pads filling with Finnish adventure as he jangled home on the train. What he would not speak about World War II worked up a sweat in the Winter War. The young captain aged into an author, loosing language as he'd once liberated a prison camp.

He wrote into the long night. He printed four hundred pages from his typewriter. The world would never sip this vintage wine from his heart.

My cracked and chaotic heart bleeds, and language is the tourniquet. I need to do this, even when it waterboards me. I need to do this, even if it doesn't matter.

I belch forth proclamations that it matters, every furtive poem and awkward essay. I tell fearful friends to write without guile, exile expectation, trust that God is in it, the Word inside the words.

I believe, for them, that even if one person reads and rejoices, it has not been in vain. I believe that even if the one is the writer himself.

But do I believe it? Do I believe it for my ego when it's doubled over in hunger, believe that my subpar striving is still a feat of soul?

If we include my mother and my big-eyed aunt, my personal essays have four readers, four electrons, four lunar orbiters circling the hoarding house of my head. My work blog has up to a thousand a day, which is terrifying and satisfying and not the point.

The meeting is the point.

This is where the sacred and profane stagger through peace talks, walking laps around language, throwing grapes into each other's mouths. This is where past and present wrestle in the dust, throwing each other's hips out of joint.

This is where I take life by its frayed edge and shake it like a picnic blanket, preparing a soft place to lay in the grass.

This is where I play, even when it feels like gulag toil, even when I would rather be back in 1986.

This is the February forsythia, lean and unready, bundled in my mother's graceful arms. Forced into warmth, it will bloom. It will tell the story that winter is on the run.

I will run this course with lunatic devotion, taking the hem of story's garment. It may be read by four or zero. It may be dreck or divine mercy. It may heal my history or fuel my fierceness.

The kingdom of love is here in the alphabet soup, and I will take it by force.

One Late October Eve
by Lynette Esposito

The dark night
streams filaments of her indigo curls
across the frosty sky.
Embellished with stars,
loosened locks shower
the late evening with tiny interwoven knots
threading the curved dome tightly together.

The translucent plaits seem to shiver
in the crisp air.

I walk home not minding my path
-- look up-- watch,
wait
for one to unravel or to fall
and undo the whole thing.
Morning comes--
the star- lit night is gone.

How to Tie a Monkey's Fist
by RJ Equality Ingram

With both hands reach into middle school
Use one thumb to hold off effervescence
While the other digs around the backyard
Looking for your eye that went missing
That one August after the car accident
Wrap the main sheet around your palm
Three times then shift your perspective
While you watch your brother sail through
The finish line winning another regatta
The trick to jealousy is to tie it into a hobby
Let him fill his hull w/ trophies & ribbons
While you quietly wait for puberty to end
Before pulling the ends slip a little secret
Into the center of the fist no one will know

11.39
by Ben Macnair

The Last Train is sleeping now,
her keeper has locked her safely away.
The last drinkers have left the pub,
and are watching the drift
as their unsteady walk
guides them home.
The rain keeps me company,
as does the Hedgehog
that slowly crosses my path,
he is a spiky football
with a mind of his own.
The last Train driver is walking home,
there is a caller on the late- night radio,
saying he heartily disagrees with any opinion,
that is not his own,
but he is only talking to the sleepless,
The ticking clock, and the chime of the bell
show another day has passed,
under this November sky.

HISTORIC
IRVINGTON
NE KNOTT ST

spin casting
by Mark DeCarteret

not that there's a reef or fish left
that figured in the last of our dreams, ate

whichever lore the fisherman
pitched from the clouds too over our heads

& we could count on like gold sheep to sink us
within an inch of that coldest & deepest of sleeps

where even the waters no longer
thirst for their own version of blood

Onset

by Yuan Changming

"What's your earliest memory?" asked Ming.

"Why are you asking me this?" Hua said.

"Because it marks the beginning of your life as a human."

"You're saying my pre-memory life is not a human one at all?"

"Not in the sense that you're a self-conscious individual."

"Well, you may have a point there…. As far as I can recall, it was in a quite busy street, where I was somehow lost, but I managed to cross it on my own, just by following other people, before my dad found me."

"When and where was that exactly?"

"In Wuchang's Horseviewing Square, when I was almost three. My father later told me that's the first time he took me for a visit to my grandpa."

"No wonder you're lost and re-found by me, at least in love."

"You mean my earliest memory set a pattern for my life?"

"Yeah, as I see it, whatever mental image is embedded in our earliest memory functions like a mythic seed, which would grow, bloom, and bear fruit in a cyclic fashion."

"What's your first memory then?"

For Ming, this was a one-million-dollar question. While he felt amazed at the fact that his soulmate had such an early and clear memory about her toddling experiences, he could recall little about his life before he was five. He had discussed the matter with his parents quite a few times, but neither was sure about the dates concerning the several situations stored in the closet of his mind.

One earliest memory was about him plodding along behind his mother, with a silver wooden sword hung on his waist, on a street in New Rivermouth on a rainy afternoon. In another mental image, he was playing a game with a group of children all living in the same residential area of the County's Finance Department. It was a warm and moony evening. Every participant pretended to be a parent. To imitate older children, he and the youngest girl of Uncle Fu, the department head, reached into each other's crotches and made a stir there with their hands. A third episode took place when he was chased around by a boy a couple of years older with a disabled hand. Just as he tried to cross the threshold, Ming stumbled and hit his head against a brick.

Most vivid was his memory about a marble he had used to have. To him, the transparent ball with something green in its heart looked particularly fascinating because it was like a tender spout encapsulated within a magic glass kaleidoscope. On a cloudy morning, he went to the backyard, dug a little hole with his fingers, and put the marble into it, wishing it would grow into something really big. However, each time he checked the place eagerly, he was disappointed that the marble had shown no growth of any kind.

"Which one was exactly your earliest memory?" asked Hua.

"I can never tell. The only thing I knew was these were my earliest memories before my parents sent me to Lotus Village as a foster child.

"You should try to figure it out with your mother's help while she's still alive or before she lost her memories."

"That's one of the reasons I've come to visit her now in such a hurry."

Once his earliest memory was confirmed, he would gain a better and deeper understanding of his life. To him, a different mental image represented a different paradigm that had somehow manifested itself repeatedly, each time in a different way, in the course of his life. For instance, the chase picture might well be taken as a symbolic precursor to his grown-up life full of hard pursuits and serious injuries. Similarly, his memory about the pretending game could perhaps help him to understand his relationships with women.

"What if your first memory was about the marble?"

"That would account for why imagination and dreaming about growth have played such an important part in my existence. Just as my physical life has been a long process of chasing and getting hurt, my spiritual life is full of wishful thinking and disappointment."

"Famous last words," said Hua.

"Maybe," Ming replied, "but that's my way to interpret my life experience, to know myself."

"If your theory is valid, then I'm fated to constantly cross a street, a helpless situation, all by myself."

"Isn't that the case? You are a brave and fortunate girl, in love, as in life."

More Sounds of Silence

by Ken Gosse

My muses have amusing ways
of teasing me on silent days
by giving me no words to write
until I try to sleep at night
then hide the notepad I keep near
and dry my pen so that no tear
of ink will cry upon the page,
thus leaving me a nightmare's rage
which twists my dreams in nasty knots
of dreadful and outrageous plots,
too strange to write and too obscure
to last till dawn—they won't endure
the hapless, napless hours tossed
until I wake, when all are lost.

Grandson at Almost Three
by Lynette Esposito

When Lucian, not yet three, puts his hand in mine.
I feel such joy--
this boy
knots his lifeline to mine
in a faith
that he can lead me to where ever he wants to go,
and I in the same perfect grandma faith,
take him there.

BIOS

KAI BROACH
Kai Broach writes fiction and poetry. Their work has appeared in *Jeopardy* and *Scribendi* magazines, and they are the winner of the 2022 Western Regional Honors Council Award for Short Fiction. They grew up around Washington's Puget Sound and currently live in Portland, Oregon, where they offer literary and bathroom advice to the customers of Powell's Books.

YUAN CHANGMING
Yuan Changming grew up in rural China and has published 15 poetry collections in English. Early in 2022, Yuan began to write fiction, with short stories appearing in *Bewildering Stories* (Canada), *Lincoln Review* (UK), *Paper Dragon* (US), and *StylusLit* (Australia), among others. Currently, Yuan is working on his trilogy.

MICKEY COLLINS
Mickey ~~rights wrongs~~. Mickey ~~wrongs rites~~. Mickey writes words, sometimes wrong words but he tries to get it write.

MARK DECARTERET
I've worked at Water Street Books in Exeter NH nearing 11 years. Stroudwater in Portsmouth NH for 7, Sheafe Street in Portsmouth for 5, and Wordsworth in Cambridge MA for 1, as well as a holiday stint at Boston University.

LYNETTE G. ESPOSITO
Lynette G. Esposito, MA Rutgers, has been published in *Poetry Quarterly*, *North of Oxford*, *Twin Decades*, *Remembered Arts*, *Reader's Digest*, *US1*, and others. She was married to Attilio Esposito and lives with eight rescued muses in Southern New Jersey.

ROBERT EVERSMANN
Robert Eversmann works for *Deep Overstock*.

KEN GOSSE
Ken Gosse prefers writing short, rhymed verse with traditional meter and generally full of humor. First published in *The First Literary Review–East* in November 2016, since then in *Pure Slush*, *Lothlorien Poetry Journal*, *Academy of the Heart and Mind*, and others. Raised in the Chicago suburbs, now retired, he and his wife have lived in Mesa, AZ, over twenty years,

usually rescue cats and dogs underfoot.

Paul Hostovsky

Paul Hostovsky's poems have won a Pushcart Prize and two Best of the Net Awards. He makes his living in Boston as a sign language interpreter.

RJ Equality Ingram

RJ Equality Ingram is a poet from Vermilion, Ohio who lives in Portland, Oregon & works as a bookseller for Goodwill Industries of the Columbia Willamette. RJ Received his MFA in creative writing with concentrations in poetry & creative nonfiction from Saint Mary's College of California & has work published in *White Stag, Pinwheel Journal, Alice Blue Review, Dreginald* as well as others. RJ's cat Brenda lost a leg in an RSVP to the prince's ball. Follow @RJEquality

Aletha Irby

My name is Aletha Irby and I have been writing poetry for over fifty years. My work has been published in *Main Street Rag, Lady Blue Literary Arts Journal, VOLT, Shot Glass Journal, Palo Alto Review, Tiny Lights Online*, and many other journals.

Ben Macnair

Ben Macnair is an award-winning poet and playwright from Staffordshire in the United Kingdom. Follow him on Twitter @ benmacnair

Timothy Arliss Obrien

Timothy Arliss OBrien (he/they) is an interdisciplinary artist in music composition, writing, and visual art. He has premiered a range of music from opera to film scores to electronic ambient projects. He has published several books of poetry, (*The Queer Revolt, Dear God I'm a Faggot, & Happy LGBTQ Wrath Month*), and has written for Look Up Records (Seattle), and *Deep Overstock*: The Bookseller's Journal. He also founded the podcast & small press publishing house, The Poet Heroic, and founded the digital magic space The Healers Coven. He also showcases his psychedelic makeup skills as the phenomenal drag queen Tabitha Acidz.
Find more at: www.timothyarlissobrien.com

James G. Piatt

James is a retired professor and octogenarian. He is a twice Best of the Net nominee and four-time Pushcart nominee. He has had five poetry books, *The Silent Pond, Ancient Rhythms, LIGHT, Solace Between the Lines,* and *Serenity*, 1775 poems, five novels, and thirty-five short stories published in scores of national and international magazines, anthologies, and books. He

earned his doctorate from BYU, and his BS and MA from California State
Polytechnic University, SLO. He lives in Santa Ynez, California, with his wife
Sandy, and a dog named Scout. His great, great aunt and uncle, Sarah
Morgan Bryan, and John James Piatt were prolific poets in the 1800s.

Jihye Shin
Jihye Shin is a Korean-American poet and bookseller based in Florida.

Emily J. Schnipper
Emily J. Schnipper (she/her) sells nature books to the people of Portland
when she is not reading, writing, or acting as hype person for the California
Condor. A graduate of the Independent Publishing Resource Center's
Portfolio Program in Poetry, she is currently working on a MFA at Pacific
Northwest College of Art. Emily is the creator of the zine *Adventures in
Unemployment* and has been published in *Ghost Print*, *Minto Press*, and
Papeachu Review. Her chapbook, *Bother*, focuses on themes of relationship,
chronic illness, and the environment.

Rin Stone
My name is Rin Stone, and I'm a trans guy from Alabama living in Portland,
Oregon. I work at Powell's City of Books where I specialize in Autistic and
queer books. Most of my writings are songs, poetry, or journal entries about
experiencing the world as a queer Autistic person.

Angela Townsend
As Development Director for a cat sanctuary, Angela bears witness to mercy
for all beings. She has an M.Div. from Princeton Theological Seminary and
B.A. from Vassar College. Angie has lived with Type 1 diabetes for 32 years,
giggles with her mother every morning, and delights in the moon. Her work
has appeared or will be published in upcoming issues of *The Amethyst
Review*, *Braided Way*, *Feminine Collective*, *LEON Literary Review*,
MockingOwl Roost, *Star 82 Review*, and *The Young Ravens Literary Review*,
among others. Angie loves life dearly.

Z.B. Wagman
Z.B. Wagman is an editor for the *Deep Overstock Literary Journal* and a co-
host of the Deep Overstock Fiction podcast. When not writing or editing he
can be found behind the desk at the Beaverton City Library, where he finds
much inspiration.

Nicholas Yandell
Nicholas Yandell is a composer, who sometimes creates with words instead
of sound. In those cases, he usually ends up with fiction and occasionally

poetry. He also paints and draws, and often all these activities become combined, because they're really not all that different from each other, and it's all just art right?

When not working on creative projects, Nick works as a bookseller at Powell's Books in Portland, Oregon, where he enjoys being surrounded by a wealth of knowledge, as well as working and interacting with creatively stimulating people. He has a website where he displays his creations; it's nicholasyandell.com. Check it out!